Love Poems For The Hopeful Romantic

Lola Blyth

ISBN: 9798734040362

DEDICATION

To all of the Hopeful Romantics and to all the beautiful
people who are once again kind enough to read my words,
this book is for you.

Wedding Bells Sing For You

Not all dreamers dream of a wedding day,
but for those who do, it forms rainbows so strong
that they cross each forest path of the mind
spreading like endearing wildfire, with easily
accessible images created for every moment, so
pristine that you're holding your future in your
own accomplished palms.

I have it all planned out already:

Belvoir
Horse and Carriage
Late Afternoon

Traditional but handcrafted with a slice of
last century that spreads softly and makes its
way into every haven of the ceremonial body,
home comforts that remind us who we are.

Lovesong.

Bouquets of flowers with white lace bonded
together with embroidery thread to reflect the
colours of our world that we share,
with enough alteration to make it memorable
just by colour, but classic enough to still feel
like a fairytale wedding so many of us have
always dreamed of but that only the paths of
The Romantics have us destined to reach.

The sun is in Leo and the air is ripe and
chimes softly as the wind catches her breath
and the clouds hide their expression
only if for a day
polka dots and hair ties coincide with the bright
smiles and warm afternoon laughs,
Twistin' The Night Away.

Sun chasers
Star gazers

The cosmos too are celestial guests,
the ones who decided that today would be
The Day,
the windows winking with sunlight,
the sunrays' waterfall current glowing vividly.

Married by Mother Nature.

This is all within my destiny,
the planets and her stars have told me so,

So here I am,
writing the future
and dreaming into existence as I speak.

Pride And Love Go Hand In Hand

To be given a label to stable your identity
and to fit the box that society tops
and says you should call it your destiny

We see the belief that we must choose
a category to be valued
and that that's what we are to do
in order to become true and valued

The people say that freedom
is to strive and to thrive
with self-treason

But you are the universe's magic.

Aphrodite
Adonis

Your power is yours and the universe
is incapable of mistakes
in its careful craft called Creation

Venus and Mars and Mercury
made you in their image
creating you from their stardust,
divine counterpart to the constellations

Claim your clamshell
travel far and wide, setting no limits
to your destination or to your stops
along the way

Freedom comes from harmony
from feeling warmed by your own fire, and thriving
in your own spark
learning the love that can be found in natural beauty,
letting yourself find comfort in your energy,
discovering that not all fire is dangerous

Chained to nothing and to nobody,
master of your own journey,
begin to escape that box,
continuing to follow no one else's rules but yours.

My Home is Flora's Temple

In the first week of Aries season
I went searching for somewhere
that would deliver flowers to
the doorstep every month,
not for anyone else but me
not for any other reason but benevolence.

My home is Flora's temple now.

The summer never backs down here,
petals light up
vacant with sunlight,
the leaves tattooed by its rays.

A celebration of myself
Benevolence to myself
A Song Of Myself.

Water moon
Natural-born nurturer
Colourful flowers to suit
a colourful personality.

The vase is seduced by the brightness,
the glass winking under the sun's charm
as the flowers breathe spring's pheromones
from their lips.

The Charm Of The Night

We stood that night in front of the stars
on the night of the full moon as she
stared down at us,
brimming with all of the passion that she garnered
in her dutiful month of waxing.

She works on her own accord,
the stars fluttering all around her,
deep in submission to her.

The wizardry and witchery of the stars
tie us together with magic ribbons that
they too were made from, and the same stardust
we were made from came from the night sky

We fell hopelessly into the charm of the night
and as we stood there, we realized that
there are constellations not only in the sky
but within ourselves too.

We came to realise that it's our own internal
clockwork of constellations that drew us together
in the first place since you cannot have a working
clock
without the mechanics inside

The nighttime has always been a surging part
of our identity
our love for celestial nature is what drew us together
whilst we were still apart
something we had in common before knowing each
other for the first time in this lifetime.

We are both children of the stars
always looking to them for guidance
always learning from the lessons they teach us
proud that we've found their wisdom and
that we navigate our lives using the most
powerful force of nature,
relaxing as we know that the stars have faith in us
and that's that' the only faith we need to survive
we are the result of their passion project.

We stood that night in front of the stars
under the full moon
in a perfect silence that captured the pure
awe and infatuation that we share
between each other and between the universe.

Letters To a Familiar Stranger

I sat by the window one time
Underneath the candlelight
Writing love letters to the one I had yet to meet
My own definition of romance
A self-date night
Planning to give them to you a few months
After we met for the first time

I sat and wrote a thousand words which
Couldn't even express to you all the things
I wanted you to know,
so much to say to you and yet I wasn't sure
of what you looked like, the sound of your voice
or the familiarity of your home.

I kept them all in the top drawer
Some written in burning red ink,
Others dated and written on colourful
Craft paper, knowing that with each letter,
The closer I grew to knowing you.

And so I repeated myself until
I reached a state of haziness and drowsiness

With each letter,
The closer I grew
To knowing you

With each letter, the closer
I grew to knowing you

With each letter, the closer I
Grew to knowing you

With each letter, the closer I grew to knowing you

With each letter, the closer I grew to finding you.

Sometimes The Next Best Thing is to Follow Your Own Path

In recent years there has been an emphasis
That every road should lead to the same place,
Self sufficiency
But nature says differently
She says that the goal is to co-exist
Since not all stars are part of the same universe
Their energies are all different
But they make it work

Without those constellations
We would cease to be where we are now,
The eclectic mix of Mars and Mercury,
Is what keeps us in rotation.

Each of us have our own personal mixture
of energies and asteroids and planets.
you have your own authority to decide your
journey.
you are the leader of your own fate and energy is
only important in the moment.
you can always change your energy,
and you can always make your own rules.

Afterall, no one said you won't find any pathways
along your walk of life.

Honeymoon Phase For Eternity

With you in my life,
the skies are always clear,
no black clouds and the only rainy days
are the showers that nature brings with her
to keep the world alive and to keep the leaves on the
trees breathing,
regenerating the flowers and giving them a pulse
that beats strong and grows as they stretch up towards
the morning star,
and during each storm that she hurls to the
rest of the world, we stay true to the eye each time
using the rain to our advantage,
bathing in it, using it to nourish all that we belong to
letting us strengthen our heartbeats and using the
droplets to dance under umbrellas like we always
wanted to do, even before we found each other.

There is no bad weather when we're together
our past and present teaches us that happiness
does not have to end and that there do not have to be
hurricanes or thunder or lightning for us to
find our feet together or to survive, as we are two
peaceful patient people who have had the word
"serenity" lodged safely deep inside our beings for
our whole lives now.

Our peace will last forever
not because we'll hide our forest fires or our
tornadoes,
But because we mastered the art of always leaving the
match unlit.
Hurricanes are not welcome here.

Heaven does not have to come from pain or from
being a fallen angel.
Heaven simply exists
Within us,
Between us,
Around us.

Forever.

The Lust of Life

Love lives long in small spaces
in the little things
in the ordinary parts of the day that become
some of the best parts of the day
only special because of togetherness
only valuable once you've found your treasure.

It grows stronger and shows itself more
in the nuances of daily life
subtle but strong
making itself known by

The many Manic Mondays
that have become the culprit of many late starts
and have been adopted by your mornings,
the rattle of tangled keys on the kitchen counter
as you both rush to reach the start of your eight
hour day.

The precise placement of pictures
and virtues collected after you collided
that promise to tell the tale of your lifetime
together,
some gifted and others handpicked between
the two of you,
memories of all your most mystical moments.

The delicately and deliberately chosen décor
that took too much time to choose,
but that you wanted perfect and a reflection
of true character as you claimed your home
as yours together.

Love lives long in small spaces
in the little things
in the ordinary parts of the day that become
some of the best parts of the day
only special because of togetherness
only valuable once you've found your forever.

Love Intertwined With The Night Sky

Come out and watch the stars with me,
let me take your arm in my hand
and guide it across our constellations
tracing the tiny fires in the exhaustive,
expansive sky.

We can go in the summer when the skies
are hopeful and the days are long but
replenishing and when we have no concept of time
because the excitement and happiness of one
another has kept our passion bright

I can show you Orion the Greek hero and show
you how to use the Sirius as a reference point
for how to find Lepus and the twelve zodiac signs
and how to find the shooting stars that met along the
same path that brought us together

You are the sky using your vastness as wisdom and
your stars as endless possibilities,
Light of the world, keeping me inspired enough to
Do as I please, encouraging me to be warmed by your
fires whilst I contemplate my next move.

No ego,
All soul.

Staring into your electrifying planets as you
Stare back into my blue moons,
Feeling the encompassing warmth of
The setting summer sun
As we feel each other's warmth caress body and soul.

Moonchildren in love with the world.

Picture of You

You smell like warm syrup
flushed with sunshine
invested in your sun sign
with me you choose to spend your time.

Euphoria.

You look like artwork,
eye of beauty
value of ruby
Yours and yours truly.

Euphoria.

You feel like summer,
Eternal warmth
Forever adored
Each other's award.

Euphoria.

You touch like lavender
Always gentle
Your hands a temple
Tender as petals.

Euphoria

You laugh like blossom,
Carefree,
At ease,
Full of serenity.

Euphoria.

Love Reflected in The Sky

We stand watching the dusk-soaked sky,
making the rest of the world surrender to us,
watching Aurora rise up past the horizon,
as her light ushers the butterflies into our
morning skies.

Our eyes stay level to the horizon,
drifting up towards the eyes of dawn,
a watercolour work of blooming statement pieces,
an eccentric morning ritual

We stay worshipping the break of day
artwork as creative as you'd find in a child's
imagination
the Morning Star's eyes on her crowd,
strangers interconnected by the same majestic
phenomenon that stays young forever,
mixing up an abundance of surprises,
new additions to her palette with every brush stroke.
the boats in the sky growing more and more
saturated as the show continues,
bolder and more daring,
pastel colours blossoming and blooming along
what seems like the edge of the skyline,
the walls of our universe.

We stand watching the remains of the vast emptiness
of the palette begin to lap up all the flowing
complexions as they reach out wider, climbing the
ceiling, slowing building its empire for the day,
something so expectedly unexpected.

As the display reaches its climax,

the starlings begin their daily ensemble,
knee deep in the magical chaos of colour,
little dancers
disappearing into one of the pockets of the sky.

I Admire You So

I admire your solidarity,
how you always stay with your face to the sun,
shutting out the shadows,
casting away the ones that don't belong to you.

Your loyalty to yourself makes me sure of
your loyalty to me.
as a lion I must take care of my pride,
and knowing your self-security makes it
a job worth living for

You've forged your own path and have stayed
faithful to it,
staying vigilant and never getting whisked into
the whirling hurricanes of others,
setting your standards high and majoring in
the art of letting go of what lies below your worth.

You've found the balance between head and heart,
learning that true wisdom comes from the guidance
of both.
you've left the weight of other people's sirens far
estranged from you,
mended your own heart and immunised yourself
from falling victim to those who try and wound you.

You're a gifted mind with a talented heart,
mastering things thought to be near impossible to
do in one lifetime, and with
a lot of love to give, you share it equally between the
rest of the world and feed some sweetness back into
your own heart and veins.
Born with bright ideas,

nothing compares to the way that your abstract,
unique but courteous and compassionate mind works.

Sky-Scraper
Bold-Decision-Maker.

I admire you for the person you've become,
it took you lifetimes to get to where you are now,
and for the rest of the journey,
I will continue to grow with you.

The Simplicity of Harmony

With you there's no idealisation,
life together is nothing short of true bliss,
your perfection comes in who you are,
not how far you reach to meet a certain
standard created by our culture,
but just in all of the elements of your
identity combined

Right place, right time
Head towards the sunshine

Everything in this moment is how it should be
how it was manufactured to start and end
and how it was made by us as a contribution
of our destiny.

Master creators
Soul chasers

Minds in flight as we become the pioneers
of our futures
intricate puzzle pieces bonded together
at the heart

Unbreakable
Totally unshakable

Our strength within ourselves is contagious,
spreading far and wide across each other's
oceans,
the strength of our wings reinforced by
each other's company

Eternal tranquility
Perfect compatibility

Our ever-growing love for each other
Still makes my heart flutter

Dance With Me

Let's dance under the rain made of fairytales,
under an umbrella made of wishes and romance.
take my hand, lift me onto my tiptoes,
spin with me under the droplets of the daytime sky

Lavishing under the clouds,
there is no true darkness here,
the shade of the sky is merely
an illusion with the true symbol being the periodic
release of abundance gathered by the heat of the
clouds

The sweet temptation of the sweetness of the water
calls out to us,
begging for admiration and inviting us to continue
moving majestically under the yellow umbrella of
the visions we never once lost sight of

This is where we always wanted to be
unspoken dreams of the imagination drifting
freely into existence,
published into reality.

Seduced by the sounds of the downfall
and the echoes of our shared elation
the water honeying our skin
delicate and passionate and the clouds chime
and charm their way over our heads
any darkness made by the clouds replaced
by the brightness of our enjoyment
the romance in the rain we all want to experience.

As long as the rain keeps falling,

Our umbrella will continue swirling and
our hearts will continue falling harder and harder
in tune with each other

One Life, One Lover

From the moment I knew what true love meant
I knew I wanted to find my one and only
my perfect match, my summertime.

One life to lead,
One lover to find.

A somewhat traditional idea that has begun
to drift away with the fast-paced ideals and standards
of society, and fast-changing conclusions of what's
possible and what's no longer the way of our world.

One life to lead,
One lover to align.

To fall in love with a single person in your lifetime
and to stay in love for all the time that you have left is
one of my biggest ambitions for the life I have to
lead.

One life to lead,
One lover to define.

They say that true love takes time to build,
and for that you must grow with different people,
or so they say
but when you've learnt to love yourself on your own
and you've experienced all the same lessons
without ever having a lover by your side,
that is when you defy gravity and teach others that
multiple lovers is an accessory, not a necessity.

One life to lead,
One lover to decide.

And so with my own wisdom and knowledge that
carries me across the vast open oceans on this
adventure of life,
I decided that my own destiny is to be fulfilled with
just one true love of a lifetime.

One life to lead,
One lover divine.

The Look of Love

How do you tell when someone's in love?
is there a new-found softness in their gaze,
or perhaps its how they carry themselves differently.

Deep, profound love is something only found
far within the pockets of the soul,
in the electricity between the static stars that
are always lit with a clean match.

When you spark someone else's fire,
and come to join them,
finding yourself in their warmth,
you let the shadows and the darkness fall
behind you,
bouncing off each other's light

Your energy field becomes theirs,
magnetic aura transcending all
vibrations,
and energetic partnership being the first thing
that draws you together,
before becoming two hearts in love.

High scorers in the art of compatibility
realising you knew each other better,
even before your world's collided.
the depth of your connection
already figured out

Venus and Jupiter created you both
giving you guidance on who they would be
a sense of familiarity
that only you would see

Knowing them like you know they sky is blue
inside and out before they even met you,
a couple making the perfect two.

Happy Ending

Your biggest talent within is that if you dream
deep enough into the profound oceans of your
thoughts, and become the catering waiter
to every ounce of your imagination,
then you will get your happy ending that your heart
has always yearned for.

For the love that you've cast a spell for,
your power comes with your ability to dream
and the fruits of your imagination give way
to the magic you've casted in your mind's eye.

The sweetest gift of the mind is the ability
to protect the labour of your visons as you
dream them up.

You may reveal your insights to those around you
but the true details and the furnishings can
all remain a part of your secret plan

What starts out as innocent dreaming, using
what the universe gave you can be the meal
of future,
it comes from dreaming and daring and dancing
your mind around all of the possibilities

Sometimes what you see is more than just
a thought.
sometimes it is the true gateway to your destiny and
what is to follow if you choose one thing or another.

Part of the power is that if you don't like the paths
your mind has made up for you,

You can simply erase and create what you want to see
your heart knows best,
and once you've finalised those dreams,
your mind and your imagination shall follow.

You will get your Happy Ending.

Summer's Heaven

One day in the peak of summer's heartbeat,
the two of us took a trip to an open meadow
full of wildflowers, deep passionate skies
and the feeling of an affectionate charm in the air.

The warmth was still persistent and the sun
was still golden,
but the sky was slowly preparing for her
evening summer spectacular, with certain shades
already creeping in from the distant horizon.

The two of us sat together,
breathing in and basking amongst the softening
sunlight as it encompassed us into her haze,
framing us as though we were a part of her collage
for the day,
a memory for you and I to hold together eternally.

The checkered blanket grounded us,
bringing us closer together into each other's comfort,
making us smile out of love, admiration and pure
beauty.

A moment of perfect silence lay between us
as we absorbed the perfection of each other
And the ever-growing romance between us

Moments later, more smiles, more laughter.
everything is brighter when I'm with you,
everything is more colourful when you're with me.
our days are filled with gratitude that we've found
each other.

The cutlery and crockery – all pastel vintage-style
china reflects the streams of sunlight pouring onto us,
plates spreading a warm current along the blanket.

Fresh flowers carefully hand chosen and picked with
precision elegantly lay amongst the plates
let their petals begin to sparkle and gleam under the
sunshine, enjoying the light as much as ourselves.

Cake stands integrated with fresh fruit flushed with
the fragrance of summer to make pleasing to the eye a
variety of replenishments, with the favourites picked
especially for each other.
pastel pink twirls of vanilla frosting glinting slightly
under the heat,

As the sun descends, our new-found heaven sparkles
passionately, glowing precociously, framed by
nature's spotlight.

We continued to sit into the dusk,
admiring each other's beauty,
watching the remaining sun rays flourish on our skin,
knowing that moments like those are the definition of
true, unconditional love.

The Value of Sentimentality

I bought a jar and kept it in the bottom of
The top drawer,
Planning gin advance for the sentiments
And the memories that would later be shared
Between the two of us,
A benchmark for our story,
A sacred place for you and I to visit
For whenever we want to soak up the best times

I wish for this jar to fill quickly,
So much buried beneath those glass walls
That upon reflection, we rediscover moments
Near impossible to remember with such a high
Volume and such a surplus mixture

When the jar is full,
We can choose a safe haven as a home for it
Perhaps for if we ever find ourselves apart,
Craving our warmth and connection,
Or simply for the leaves of happiness
If gifts us with

Perhaps then we can use something bigger
A real life treasure chest,
A unit to collect the memories of a full,
Love-filled lifetime together,
A blessing for the children of our future
For them to look back on trying to decide
Their own definition of eternal love.

We'll write as we go,
Recording the very first endearments of each other,
Hearts, minds and souls alike

All captured in one glass jar.

Fruit Pickers

The height of summer calls for
Another adventure.
We find ourselves deep among the fruit bushes,
Flowers blooming for us.

Petite woven baskets swung over our hands,
With our arms in each other's,
Feeling the gentle pulse of the heat,
Whose arousal by the wind grows prominent

The tradition of it doesn't take away from the
Bliss of it all
You and I could do the same thing one hundred times
And it would still hold more value than any precious
stone.

The strawberries are all burning with the same shade
Of red, bold with enthusiasm,
The sunlight reflecting some of the red back onto
Your face,
Confirming your place as a Renaissance painting.

The birds hum and the bees are preoccupied with
Nature's cycles, letting the outside world melt
Around them.
We watch them, closer still, fascinated by their drive
And ambition to their own small kingdom.

We pick the strawberries, one by one,
Each warm to the touch in the palm of our hands,
As they spotlight themselves, pleading to be freed
From the arms of their bushes.
As the fruit falls freely but firmly into the baskets,

The more I freely and firmly fall for you.

Tea For Two

Pretty pink pastel plates punctuate the table,
As pruned petals please the eye, littered like
Spontaneous brushstrokes crawling across
Paper.

Tones of burning reds and pinks blush in tune
With the rising sun and her clouds,
Creating the perfect composition.

The perfection in this time dedicated to each other
Makes itself known by the tranquility we inhale and
the
Affection we lick up.

A time to spend just as the two of us,
Before the traffic of the outside world
Steals us away.

The morning after a night under the stars
And the lace tablecloth begins to sway
Hypnotically in tune with the wind.

As the sun rises,
The shadows fall behind us,
Allowing the flower displays to climb for the light.

The teapot's chimney whirrs, being brought to life as
you tilt it towards the mouth of a teacup,
Steam escaping rapidly but gracefully into the
Calm abyss we partnered with mother nature to
Create.

The temperature picks up,

And we begin to talk the day towards us,
Pinpointing our many curiosities,
Discussing our dreams, wishes and wonders.

The Bookshelf

The bookshelf stretches out far and wide
Enough material to supply someone with
A lifetime of wisdom, teaching them
Lessons in the form of knowledge.

The meeting point for an honouring mixture of
genres,
All woven together to make the unique
Selection where each book forms the perfect
Compliment to the next,
Each book chosen with ultimate care and love,
Some stories part of the structure of the bookshelf,
Others becoming a more recent addition but
Treasuring just as much value as the rest.

The Bookshelf has an established structure,
Its base in fine feather,
With a space that's always growing,
Able to house
more wisdom, more stories, more memories,
with a continuous and permanent accommodation.

The Bookshelf consists of a
colourful exterior, and a rooted, rich interior,
A shattering happiness and a soothing disposition,
The books well maintained, the shelves frequently
Dusted, book jackets always protecting.

The books supporting one another,
But not weighing each other down,
But more so keeping each other tall, grounded and
Boundlessly supported,
Pages embracing each other,

Book covers bonding with each other.

Star-Crossed Lovers

Made for lovers was the melodrama
and the dramatic pulse and heartbeat
of the stars.

Lovers belong to the fires in
the nighttime skies,
the waxing moon each night laps them up
and lifts them high into her arms.

Silent stalker
Night watcher

The stars parade for the sake of romance,
making themselves known to the hopeful romantics
that lie below their blanket,
millions of planets away.

There's a constellation made just for them,
off to the east of Orion,
the star-crossed lovers
given to us by Vega in Lyra's constellation.

The sun and the moon model for us,
the sun rises each day to allow the moon
to absorb and reflect her light,
teaching us that the perfect complimentary pair
should be the satellites for all of their gifts and all of
the talents that the universe bestowed upon us.

Look close enough and you may also see
that once you fix your eyes on the beauty
of the skies,
the velvet night will pull away her white blindfolds,

allowing you take a look at her glinting gemstones,
the source of your very existence,

the home of your soul.

The Great Escape

Let's get out,
Diffuse all our worries and stresses
Out of blood

It will be like The Great Escape,
A dramatic flair to keep us on our toes,
Enough to distract us from the continuous
Engine of the human traffic,
And from all of the man-made errands
And responsibilities.

Perhaps we could find a cottage somewhere,
Take all the cliché walks in the woods and
Fall into the stereotype of spending time in nature,
Collecting wildflowers to craft our own bouquets
To take home and arrange on the kitchen counter,
Leaving behind inconclusive trails of pollen.

Feeling weightless, happiness so outstanding
That our feet no longer touch the ground,
Colliding with Artemis as we venture
Further and further into a tangible,
Determined ether.

The song of simplicity is sweet
It lets us leave everyone who knows
Anything about us behind,
Leaving us to create whoever we choose to be,
Allowing us to breathe different air,
Lost deep in the abyss

We could do anything we wanted,
The world and her pearls are all ours

For the taking.

Or maybe,
we could stay just here in the comfort of sweet
familiarity and hometown adventures.

The Pearl And its Clamshell

Together we make the perfect duology
one pearl and one clamshell,
living harmoniously under an ocean
made of fairytales,
Poseidon and Aphrodite,
deep serenity,
fruits of the ocean

Immortal from the sands of time
captains of our own souls,
masters of our stories
realism intertwined with soft magic

Rule makers
Rule breakers

No time for demise
for here the water carries the life in us,
the story of the end is rewritten
a homely peace surrounds each surface
bubbles grounding us in this vast
open space

Rulers of the ocean,
rising among the lightness of the waves
powered by the persuasive droplets of the moon
and the collaboration of the elements,
floating in the promised grace of
the gates of the seabed

Drawing in breath by breath,
held tightly by the sole of the waves above,
The clamshell claps its pearl,

In a state of perfect, protected stillness

Illusions of Time

I held a rose quartz stone in my hand
Channeling myself to you
The stone warming in the nighttime
Of my palms,
Envisioning a wonderland of my own imagination

Shaping my thoughts one by one
Creating the perfect romance between
Celluloid scenes and the power of
The human mind

Sending whispers into the restlessness
Of the cosmic atmosphere,
Translating all of the energy I can get,
Establishing a connecting between us
Finding out how much I can garner
From the distance that lies between us

A realisation is stumbled upon,
Noticing that distance is merely an illusion
Since energy has no limitations of how far
It can travel,
It can easily stretch from the end of my rainbow
To the end of yours

Our bodies are simply a vessel
Used to communicate and to
house the messages and the waves of input
sent out by our surroundings.

It takes the strength of love for two hearts to
Feel the beat of one another from far away
And to fall gently in sync with one another

But once you realise that the heart
Is the messenger and the voice only
Aids the heart in communication,
Two people are never truly apart.

Warmth In Winter

The caves of my hands always stay up
Facing towards the sun, always ready to receive
Your shipments of sentimentality in this world,
Palm lines shifting and softening as I get to grips
With the knowledge and understanding of my fate
And new-found stability and comfort half achieved
on my own and the other half met by you.

Subdued cotton filters of the earth soak up
the colours of the atmosphere,
Engulfing us in its mellowed, honeyed celluloid
scenes,
Painting us authentically since
In our world, everything is what it seems.

As the seasons shift from cool to warm,
We know that our ripeness will be complete by
summer.
In tune with state of the sky,
We stay in solidarity,
Letting the world change around us
As when summer blossoms,
We too find our completion of the year
With a warm anticipation that keeps us
Powering towards the future together
With ambition strong enough to last
Much longer than the years ahead.

Between us there is no winter
A necessary part of nature,
not one that has to be brash or harsh
But instead one that lets love grow for us,
Finding peace in solidarity

Providing ourselves with out own heat when the sun
is distant,
Through the Burning Love and passion
That maintains infatuation.

Flowers Bloom For You

Flowers bloom for you
Harmonising with the embers
Of the glowing skies,
Clouds lighting up
As you cross their path

Blossom falls for you
Showering you in a confetti
Capturing you in a congratulations
That was earned by your heart for
following the commands of the universe

Roses flower for you
Protecting you with
Their soft thorns
Displaying to you
Their vulnerable velvet petals

Trees grow for you
Spreading their leaves
Far and wide
Shading you as the sunrays
Charge the air

Dandelions fly for you
Serving up your wishes
And taking them to the sky messengers
Placing them into the
hands of the universe

Petals colour for you
painting their way
into blooming as a result

of your omnipotent energy
you spent so long balancing

Flowers bloom for you,
Harmonising with your
Blossoming beauty,
Lighting the world up
As you cross their path

Set On You

I was once a believer that experimental
Belonged to me, that it was a part of my
Journey I was sure to encounter,

Ninth house stellium
A predisposition to adventure
A sense of newness and experience

I lived with the same meaning
Translated and engraved into
Every pathway in the maze of my mind

To stick with tradition seemed dull at the time
Something of such a distant familiarity
To the changing generations

but since making that decision,
I've met my authentic self
coming to realise the fluidity
of what seemed like final options

instead I chose to do what was always there
the abstract thoughts I never paid much attention to
that if I can pick even just one clover of what I want
to happen in my journey,
then it's worth pioneering that into my existence

my heart is what knows love the best
and so by keeping an eye on the destination
of its satellites,
I came to conclude that one journey in love
is enough to give me a plentiful experience
and will still allow me to absorb what life

wants to offer me

I got to thinking that every road I take will always lead back to you.

Lucid Love

Young lovers make dreamers who
never stray away
From the side of exploration,
Never afraid of their own cosmic minds,
Never far from the strong familiarity
Of their own imagination,
Never drifting away from
their own power,
Sharing with one another
Their own bright thoughts
Feeling each other's energetic fields
From miles apart

Not bound by time or by space
Instead using the universe to
Their advantage,
As a point of connection,
Paying homage to the celestial skies
That designed their connection
And that keep their romance alight

No more cloudy dreams
For such a deep connection holds the power
For one another to take the spotlight,
Visions of the future together living on
Until they become a part of their reality

Within their benevolence,
They shift our known reality
Creating the place that has always
Between present between their minds

A place between two worlds,

A world dreamt into existence

Perhaps not for the outer population,
But just for the enrichment of the young
Dreamer's lives together

As Clear As Day

The honey of your voice flows softly
As you speak with words that can only be tasted
Each chosen with the decision to
Speak with precision
As you warm the air with elegant diction

Changing the current of your own waterfall
With each breath
Making sure it stays flowing to be attentive to
Me, but never letting waves be formed
Or letting the river run close to the rocks

Using intuition to predict the current of
My own waterfall,
Never second guessing,
Trusting within yourself

Knowing my mind as well as your own
Your empathic nature spotlighting my heart
Detecting my sentiments with your
Supersonic radar
Without me even making a sound

A soul bursting with immortality,
Passion and love to give
Freely and fondly,
A young heart that steered you towards me
And pulled our lives together

Our connection handpicked by
The fruits of the cosmos
And finalised by our will to find forever

I know that in you,
I have found the
Heart, mind and soul I have always loved.

Velvet Scenes of The Night

Molten seduction makes hard for resistance
Lured in by the power of profound adoration
Closeness making intimacy contagious

Besotted by perfection
Tenderness makes desire grow fonder,
Two souls channeling hunger between
Two bodies and two hearts

Teasing and tasting love
In the simple way of physical connection
Lovers metaphysically intertwined
Transcending past the
ultimate level of devotion

Crossing paths with all things cosmological
Lighting the match to start our personalised
Fire of admiration

Worshipping the invaluable nature of sensuality
Confident and fitted securely in all that we are
Transmuting all energy within our beings
Turning it into that of eros

A passion that grows fonder
Two souls in perfect vibrant harmony
Alignment between two people and
The sacred moments that lie before them

Hearts and eyes alike are full
Brimming with tenderness
Full moons enchanting and entertaining
A spell cast merely through existence

Mind readers in tune with the body language
Of a god and goddess,
Velvet scenes of passion
Following each other
Through the night

Swan Song

Underneath the twilight skies
Pockets of air filled with passing asteroids
Juno small but mighty
Carrying the weight of romance
Beneath her wings

The nighttime sun glowing vividly
In amongst the moon landing
Of two besotted souls
Nourishing each other
Under natural candlelight

The sky lights up for them
Each one of her celestial bodies
Replenished after craving the darkness,
Locking themselves to the pristine atmosphere

The prior day disintegrates dutifully
Laying calmly to rest
the collisions of chaos
Creating clearer visions for
Tomorrow's journey

The nightfall grows thicker
Busking to the cosmic currents
Of the besotted souls
Beneath them

Time comes undone in the night sky
No pressure or dilemma
Or single moments
Only the power of space
And nature's comforts

And the two besotted souls

Side by side
In the arms of the night